Santa's
Christmas Surprise

Santa's
Christmas Surprise

By Robert Bernardini
Illustrated by James Rice

PELICAN PUBLISHING COMPANY

Gretna 1994

The word "Pelican" and the depiction of a pelican are trademarks
of Pelican Publishing Company, Inc.,
and are registered in the U.S. Patent and Trademark Office.

Library of Congress Cataloging-in-Publication Data

Bernardini, Robert.
  Santa's Christmas surprise / by Robert Bernardini ; illustrated by
James Rice.
     p. cm.
  Summary: Santa's elves, who come from many nations and cultures,
surprise Santa and Mrs. Claus on Christmas day.
  ISBN 1-56554-089-1
  [1. Elves—Fiction. 2. Christmas—Fiction. 3. Santa Claus-
-Fiction. 4. Stories in rhyme.] I. Rice, James, 1934- ill.
II. Title.
PZ8.3.B458San 1994
[E]—dc20   94-12716
                                                       CIP
                                                        AC

Manufactured in Korea

Published by Pelican Publishing Company
1101 Monroe Street, Gretna, Louisiana 70053

T'was the morning of Christmas and at the North Pole
Not a creature was stirring, not even a mole.
Santa Claus slumbered all tucked in just right,
Resting from flying and working last night.

His little elf helpers slept snug in their beds;
One of these elves was our little friend Jed.
And in the next cottage was sweet Annabelle,
Tossing and turning and not sleeping well.

She could not get comfy in any position,
'Cuz feelings were coming from her intuition.
Finally she got up and called little Jed . . .
"I'm feeling that something is different," she said.

"Please help me check to see everyone's safe;
To make sure our friends are all snug in their place."
So at every elf house they knocked on the door,
And found twenty elves—which was all, minus four!

"Sakes alive!" Jed cried. "Now where could they be—
Jose, Tyrone, Antoinette, and Soo Lee?
They're gone from their homes and nowhere to be found.
They must have left last night with hardly a sound!"

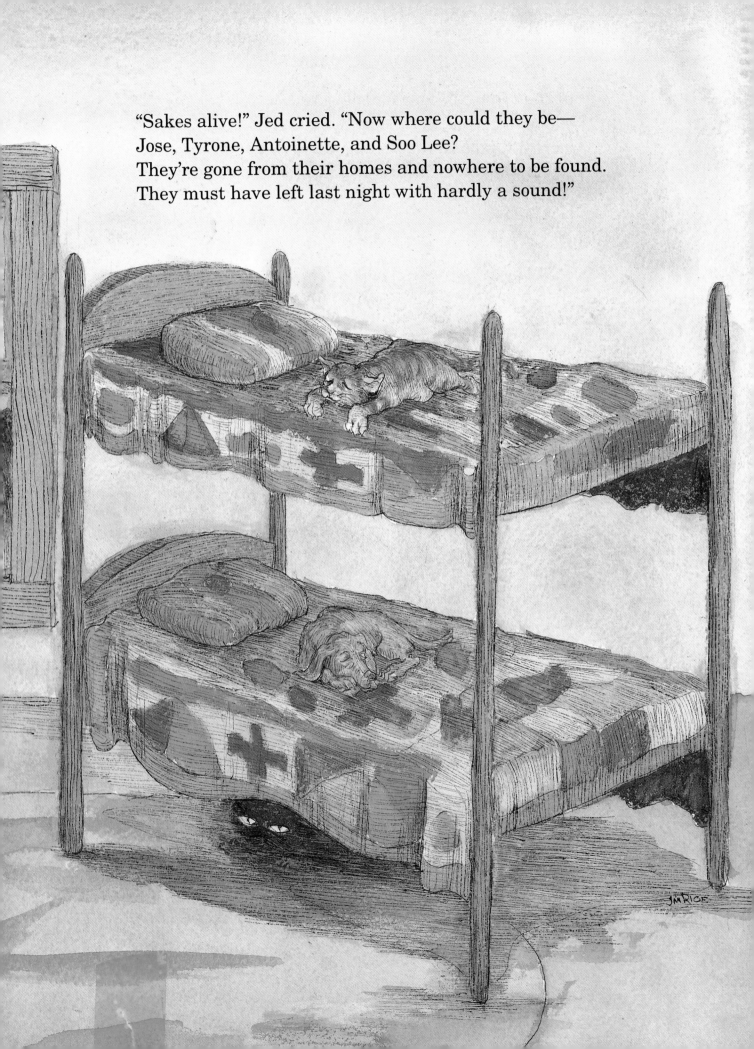

But then from the south came a sound that soon grew
Louder with time to become a *"choo-choo"!*
The North Pole Express chugged its way up the tracks,
With billows of smoke coming from its smokestack.

And from the front engine waved four little elves
Who had taken a Christmas Eve trip by themselves.
Traveling fast across the U.S.A.,
They loaded the train to the brim, you might say!

The other elves laughed and they all waved with glee,
Thankful to see they were safe and happy!
The train pulled in front of the North Pole Depot,
And everyone there wondered, "Where did they go?"

Tyrone jumped down and he said with a grin,
"My three friends and I went to visit our kin.
And each place we stopped, people gave many gifts
For us to bring back to give Santa a lift!"

Then little Soo Lee, Antoinette, and Jose
Told all of the elves what to do this fine day:
To bring all the presents into Christmas Hall
So they could surprise old St. Nick with it all!

Crates of red apples straight from the Northwest,
Freshly baked bread from farms in the Midwest,
Peaches and melons from fields way down South—
Treats that taste good and melt right in your mouth!

Pants for St. Nick and new clothes for his wife,
Candles with handles to light up the night.
Food for the reindeer to eat when it's cold,
And a special wax to shine Rudolph's red nose!

These gifts and more the elves carried inside.
They put them up high and they stacked them real wide.
Never before were gifts piled so tall
Inside that building they called Christmas Hall!

They turned all the lights out to make it real dark,
As Jed went for Santa to come on a lark.
And soon Santa Claus and his wife stood outside,
Wondering why they were wanted inside.

Santa said, "Jed, this is my day to sleep!
I flew fast all night spreading love, joy, and peace!
What could you want me to go in there for?
The hall is empty; there's nothing in store!"

Jed did not speak anymore but instead
He pulled Santa's sleeve to the door straight ahead.
Antoinette opened the door from inside;
The lights were turned on and the elves yelled, *"Surprise!"*

Santa Claus blinked as he dropped his big jaw,
Speechless and silent from all that he saw.
Then little Jose came up and he said,
"This Christmas these gifts are for *you* instead!

"The people all over the U.S. of A.
Give them as presents to you on this day!
They know how you work hard throughout the whole year,
To make sure there's plenty of Christmas-day cheer.

"And with all these presents they send you these cards,
With holiday greetings and their best regards.
They love you and thank you for all that you do,
And know that each Christmas they can count on you!"

Santa looked at everyone there inside,
With a big tear of joy welling up in his eye.
Then he gave each elf a big Christmas-day hug . . .
A Christmas-day hug filled with Christmas-day love!

Then little Soo Lee called out to everyone,
"Now is a good time to have Christmas fun!
Start up the music and let's dance and sing,
And spread all the joy that this special day brings!"

The Great Snowball Band played the carols we know.
The elves did a dance that was called "Twinkle Toes."
And Santa and Mrs. Claus sang a duet.
This day was a day they would never forget.

And later that day when the party was through,
The elves all went home to do things that elves do.
But Santa stayed in that hall thinking a while.
For *him* to get presents—now that made him smile!

So now is the right time for all of us here
To give thanks to Santa this time of the year.
And let's call real loud so he'll hear us all say . . .
"Merry Christmas, dear Santa, on this Christmas day!"